W9-AXL-545

Dear Parent:

You and your child are about to embark on an extraordinary adventure in learning!

Hello, I'm Eric Rymon! Welcome to my house! Something wild is always happening here. You and your child will enjoy yourselves as you spend time together thinking and imagining.

Like all of the exciting Rhyme Time with the Rymons books, my story, A Better Way Than Throw Away, is more than a good time. The problems we deal with in the story, audiotape, and activities are like problems real families face. Together, the story, tape, and activities teach your child things like reasoning and problem solving that are important in school.

While I was helping Mother Earth, the Thinking Well people were helping your child by adding thinking questions to my story and audiotape. These questions help your child learn from my story. They offer a chance to think about the problems and solutions in the story. They also offer a chance to talk about ideas and ask questions.

My story especially gives your child a chance to make decisions about thoughts and feelings. As in all the Rhyme Time with the Rymons stories, your child will also use imagination.

I hope your family enjoys the adventures of my family. It's Rhyme Time with the Rymons!

Your friend,

Eric

ISBN 1-55999-151-8

A division of LinguiSystems, Inc.

Other products in the Rhyme Time with the Rymons Series:

Thinking Well
3100 4th Avenue
East Moline, IL 61244

1-800-U-2-THINK

Rhyme Time with the Rymons
A Better Way than Throw Away

Story by Susan Rose Simms
Illustrated by Paul Dallgas-Frey

When Eric, Brent, and Emily
Came home from school one day,
They saw something on the sidewalk
As they passed along the way.

The garbage cans along their street
Were a familiar sight,
But these plastic bins were new.
They were so small and light.

*Do the Rymon children live far from
their school? How can you tell?*

What do you think the plastic bins are for?

"Look there," said Eric, pointing to
Three bins, each stacked on top.
"What are these for?" Brent asked
As they came to a stop.

"PAPER, GLASS, and CANS," said Emily,
Proud of the words she read.
"Hey, these are for recycling,"
Eric quickly said.

Recycling.

Paper

GLASS

cans

"What's recycling?" Emily asked.
"It's a word I haven't heard."
Brent answered, "I can tell you, Em,
Because I know that word!

"It means paper, cans, and glass
Can be reused.   It's neat!
It helps to make new paper goods,
And even repave the streets!"

recycle...?

Eric and Brent know things that Emily doesn't.
Does that mean they're smarter? Why?

Why should we reuse paper, glass, and cans?

When they got home, Chuckleberry
Met them at the door.
He barked as all three children
Threw their things upon the floor.

He went over to the corner, and
He carted out the broom.
Then he found Dad's slippers and
Removed them from the room.

Where do you think Chuckleberry took Dad's slippers?

"Hey, look at Chuck!" cried Eric.
"Maybe he has a notion
To clean up where we live,
Not just make a commotion."

Would you like to have a dog like Chuckleberry? Why?

"We all share the environment,
And ours really needs a cure.
So we need to adopt a clean up plan
To make the earth clear and pure."

"I know what 'adopt' means," said Emily.
"That's what happened after my birth.
My birth mom couldn't care for me,
Though she loved me best on earth."

"We wanted a sister," Eric said,
Filling in the rest.
"Mom and Dad chose you
Because you were the very best!"

Do Eric, Brent, and Emily
get along well?

How can you tell?

Brent said, "Now Mother Earth needs us,
To fight against pollution.
That's when there's too much trash.
There must be a solution."

The Rymon children began to wonder
What they could do in time
To help Mother Earth live longer.
Then they heard the doorbell chime.

Emily, Brent, and Eric all ran.
Chuckleberry chased them.
When they all opened the door,
Their friend, Juan Sanchez, faced them.

¡Hola, Juan!

Who is Mother Earth?

What do you think we could do to help Mother Earth live longer?

"What's up?" asked Eric of his friend.
"Tell us, Juan, what is it?"
Juan said, "My relatives from Mexico
Are coming here to visit.

"We're going out to dinner,"
And a smile lit his face.
"My parents said that I could choose
My very favorite place.

"I can't decide because I like
Hamburgers with a bun.
But at the fast food restaurants,
The tacos, too, are fun!"

If you were taking friends to dinner tonight, where would you choose to eat? Why?

Emily said, "Cafeterias are great
Because you take a tray
And stand in line to choose your food
As you walk along the way."

Why are the other customers looking at Chuckleberry?
Would you like Chuckleberrry to share his meal with you? Why?

"On special nights," began Eric,
"I like to go where waiters seat you.
When you first come through the door,
A hostess is there to greet you."

Would Chuckleberry be a good waiter? Why?

"I've got it!" yelled Eric. "We talked
About waste from paper, glass, and cans.
We can start to throw less away,
And, Juan, this could be your plan."

How could the Rymon family throw less away?
How does Eric feel about his idea? How can you tell?

"You could find a restaurant that
Helps out in all these ways –
Recycling paper bags,
And foam, and plastic trays."

Juan said, "I think I'll choose a restaurant,
Where we really ought to go,
That's concerned about recycling.
My Dad will want to know."

What does Juan think about Eric's plan?

Why do you think Juan's Dad will want to know why he chose the restaurant?

LATER...

They talked to Mom and Dad about recycling.
Mom asked, "What can OUR family do?"
"We can use cloth towels to wipe up spills."
Eric said, "And cloth for napkins, too!"

"When I get my birthday presents,"
Emily added, gaily clapping,
"I'll open them so carefully,
We can reuse the wrapping."

What are some of the ways the Rymons could reuse Emily's gift wrapping?

"Here's what we'll do," Mom said,
"Take cloth bags to the grocery store.
We'll fill them up and bring them home,
And take them back next time for more!"

"In the garage," suggested Brent,
"We'll store papers, glass, and plastic.
We'll have a place for pop cans, too.
Hey, these ideas sound fantastic!"

Why are cloth bags better for the environment than paper bags?
Why will the Rymons have four recycling bins instead of one?

AND A LITTLE LATER...

Mom and Dad said, "What a great plan!"
Chuck added his "Bow wow!"
Then Dad asked, "Where did Chuckleberry
Hide my slippers now?"

"Chuck didn't hide them," Eric laughed,
And Dad wasn't really mad.
"He was just cleaning our environment,
The place we live in, Dad!"

Think 'n' Tell

ALUMINUM CANS ONLY!

Why are there three bins for recycling paper, glass, and cans instead of just one?

GLASS

What other things could the Rymon family do to help Mother Earth?

PLASTIC

Pretend you're Mother Earth. What would you tell the people who live on earth?

PAPERS

Why is recycling important?

How could Juan find out if a restaurant practices recycling?

Trash Collector

Chuckleberry and the rest of the Rymons decided to clean their environment, the place they live in. You can use this trash collector to clean your environment!

What you need:

an empty gallon milk jug

scissors

What to do:

1. Wash the milk jug.

2. Cut a hole in the side of the jug without the handle.

3. Walk through your house or your yard and fill your trash collector with trash. Empty the trash into the correct recycling bins!

Will your trash collector work better inside or outside? Why?
Could a garbage collector use your trash collector? Why?

Recycling Rymons

The Rymon family is trying to recycle their trash. Eric thought of these two ideas that you can try.

Recycled Clothing

Does someone in your family have a shirt that they don't want? Don't let them throw it away! Use Eric's idea to recycle it!

What you need:

an old shirt

fabric paint

a piece of cardboard

What to do: Ask permission to take the shirt! Slide the cardboard into the shirt. Cover yourself with an apron and roll up your sleeves. Have fun painting your shirt!!

If your recycled shirt is too large, what can you use it for?

What can you do with a shirt that is too small?

Recycled Crayons

When you color often, your crayons get very small. They are hard to hold! Instead of throwing them away, try this recycling idea.

What you need:

small pieces of crayons without paper

small wax-coated paper cup

microwave

What to do:

1. Break crayons into very small pieces. You should only use three colors of crayon.

2. Arrange the crayon pieces in the cup so that all pieces of the same color are together.

(top view)

3. Carry the cup carefully to the microwave. Melt the crayons for 35 seconds.

4. Allow the melted crayon to cool for at least 30 minutes.

5. Carefully peel the cup off of the crayon.

How is your recycled crayon different from your regular crayons? How is it the same?

Recycle Rap

A rap is a poem that has music in the background. You don't sing a rap, you say it with rhythm. Try this rap with the Rymons.

A Better Way Than Throw Away

Let me tell you what the Rymons do
With paper, glass, and cans.
When it's time to throw 'em out,
They use a special plan.

    Listen to me now!

Recycling is the name of the game.
It's the Rymons' plan.
They don't throw away papers and glass;
They use them over again.

    Re-use it—don't lose it!

Eric, Brent, and Emily too
Work hard to eliminate waste.
By collecting cans and sorting trash,
They put things back in place.

    Put it back now!

The Rymons' plan can help save the earth
From litter, waste, and smoke.
If everybody would just pitch in,
The air won't make us choke.

    Pitch in now!

When we just toss away our cans,
We only take and take.
But if we recycle and use 'em again,
We give Mother Earth a break!

    Give her a break!